This MAMMOTH belongs to

_____

_____

_____

We're Not Tired

·Selina Young·

MAMMOTH

"Hello, I'm Ness and this is my brother, Hamish.
It's bedtime and we've put on our pyjamas.
Mum's come to tuck us in and turn out the light."

"I'm not tired," I say, when Mum's
gone downstairs.

"Let's play tents," says Hamish.
Teddy joins in too because he can't sleep either.

"But explorers quietly, so Mum won't hear."

"Hunting for buried treasure."

"Come on, let's build a rocket," I say.
"I'll be the captain and we'll fly to the moon,"
says Hamish.

"We might get captured by aliens."

"And have to fight them off."

"I'm fed up with aliens. G R R R R R.
I'm a tiger now," I say, in a very tigery way.

We go growling and prowling through the jungle.
"My tiger's knees are sore," I say.

"Let's be dancers," Hamish says.

So we ring and we rose right round the room.

We go huffing and puffing . . .

And dancing and prancing . . .

And trumpeting and tooting.

BOOM BANG!

Then SUDDENLY...

"Quick, get into bed!" I say.

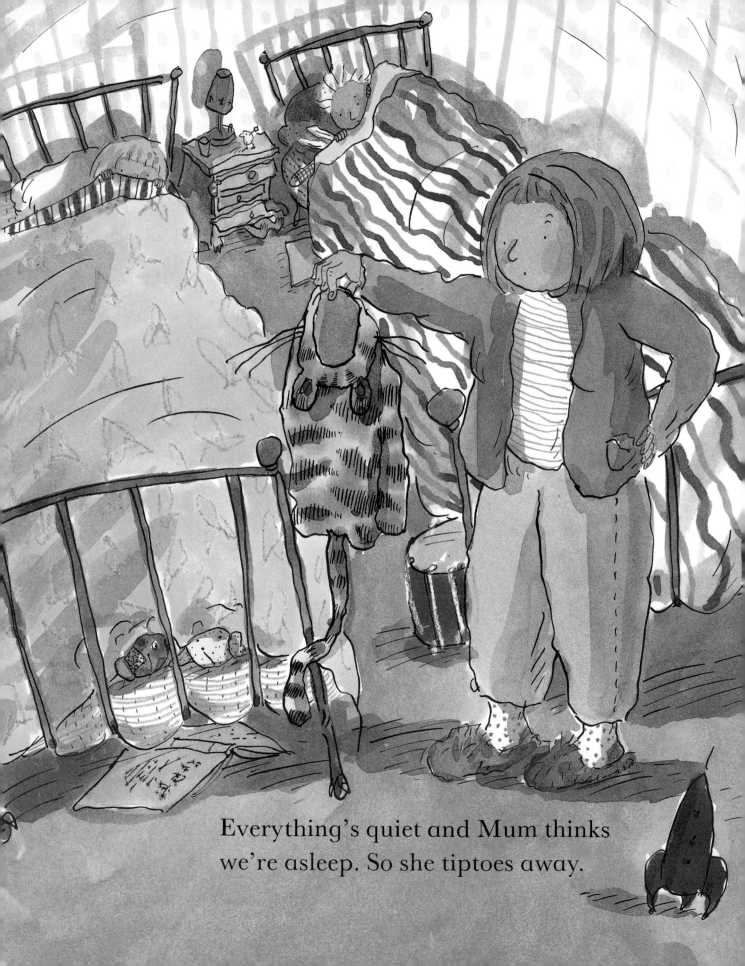

Everything's quiet and Mum thinks
we're asleep. So she tiptoes away.

"It's all right, she's gone," says Hamish.
"Let's pretend to be mice who are creeping
and squeaking."
"My mouse is thinking of sleeping," I whisper.
"Mine too."
We snuggle down deep under the covers.

"I'm tired now," I say.

"Me too," whispers Hamish.
"Let's play sleeping."

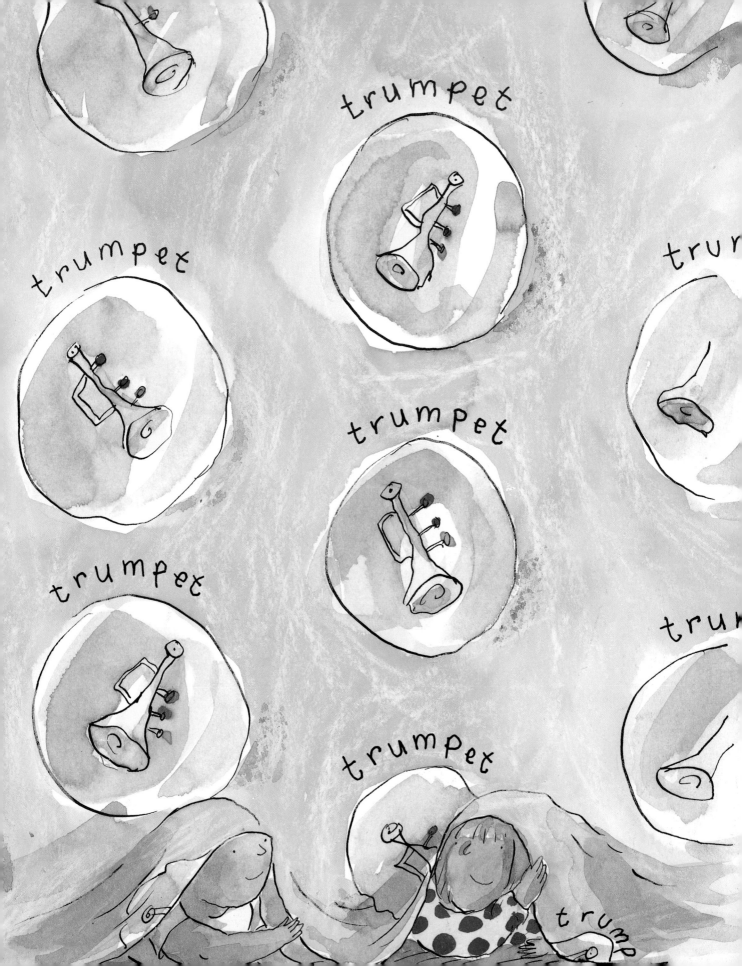

MAMMOTH

First published in Great Britain 1993
by William Heinemann Ltd
Published 1994 by Mammoth
an imprint of Reed Consumer Books Ltd
Michelin House, 81 Fulham Road, London SW3 6RB
and Auckland, Melbourne, Singapore and Toronto

Copyright © Selina Young 1993

ISBN 0 7497 1766 1

A CIP catalogue record for this title
is available from the British Library

Produced by Mandarin
Printed and bound in China